Two Boring Twin Brothers

Katelyn Halko

Copyright © 2017 Katelyn Halko

ISBN: 1979498873
ISBN-13: 978-1979498876

For Grant, my precocious first born and an amazing big brother.
And for Alex and Ben, our sweet and crazy twins that brought so much fun to our lives.

My mom is growing TWO babies in her belly. That's called twins. Our twins are boys – my new baby brothers. Mom says it's special to have twin brothers, but I'm not so sure.

Choo-choo!

When I go to the doctor with Mom, I get to hear the babies' heartbeats. It sounds just like helicopters!

Mom said I could talk to the babies too, so I got my megaphone so The Brothers could hear me better.

Grandma and Grandpa came today because The Brothers are ready to come out of Mom's belly!

I picked out a balloon for each of The Brothers and I got one for myself too, because I'm a big brother now.

When The Brothers come home, Mom and Dad are very tired because those babies eat

ALL. THE. TIME.

They even eat when it's nighttime!

Mom said she needs coffee, and Dad

sounds grumpy, and our house is

messier than Christmas morning!

I think The Brothers should go back to the hospital. Then Mom and Dad won't have to hold them all the time. Mom said it doesn't work that way.

7   8   9   10   11   12   1   2   3

She says being a big brother to twins can be hard but by the time

The Brothers turn one, I'll see just how special it will feel. Will they

be one next week? I ask. But Mom says it will take twelve long

months. So I start counting.

Month 1

These silly babies only sleep and drink milk.

Not special.

The Brothers cry. A LOT. It hurts my ears, and Mom's ears too, but she doesn't plug hers.

MONTH 3

Dad brings home so many diaper

boxes that I've built a whole train!

MONTH 4

Whenever we go on errands, strangers always ask Mom the same thing. "Are they twins? How do you tell them apart?" Hello? I'm right here too! Maybe I have invisible super powers.

Month 5

When grownups can't tell the babies apart, they always ask me. I'm an

expert on my brothers. One has an oval head and one has a round head.

The Brothers are ready to eat baby food and I get to help Mom! We give them a spoonful of slimy stuff, and they spit it right back out.

I stick out my tongue and they laugh! My brothers think I'm so funny.

Month 7

The Brothers can sit up without falling on their heads.

I wonder if they're all grown up now.

MONTH 8

Playing with The Brothers isn't always fun.

I VROOMED my car on their faces so they could see it up close, but they started crying. I threw my favorite bouncy ball to them, but it hit one in the eye.

I thought maybe they wanted a hug to make them feel better, but those silly babies fell backwards instead.

MONTH 9

These brothers are always looking for me because I'm their favorite. I'm your BIG brother I tell them and they give me slobbery kisses. I can even give them rides in the push car now!

Going places with my brothers can be fun. Their stroller is so big, there's even room for me to hop on the front when my legs are tired! Now my mom can wheel all three of us around at the same time.

You want to know something really special? At Christmas time, we all visited Santa. My brothers cried but I was so brave because I'm the biggest. And you want to know something else? Santa brought The Brothers their very own toys!

Mom says we have to start planning The Brothers' birthday party! They're almost one year old. I can't wait to see them eat their first birthday cake and get so messy.

It's been twelve long months and Mom was right - I'm glad we have twins. I can ride on their double stroller when my legs are tired. I have a back-up brother when one is crabby. Plus, I'm the twin expert when grownups can't tell them apart. Some kids only get to have one boring baby.

But I'm special. I get to be a big brother to twins!

81425832R00015

Made in the USA
San Bernardino, CA
07 July 2018